THE CAT
THAT CLUMPED

THE CAT THAT CLUMPED

by Paul Annixter

pictures by
Brinton Turkle

Published by
YOUNG READERS PRESS, INC.
New York

1st printing .... September 1969
Printed in the U. S. A.

THE CAT THAT CLUMPED

*A*LONG TIME AGO THERE WAS a family of cats that lived in a great barn. There were nine of them, and they were the slinkiest, cattiest sort of cats—all except one small kitten named Hubert. All the other cats went creeping and sneaking about the barn, hunting mice and rats. They lurked in the shadows and hardly made a sound.

But not Hubert. He was no prowl cat. He didn't want to slink or creep or hunt mice and rats. Hubert wanted to make a big important noise in the world. He wanted to clump when he walked—like the horses that lived in the great barn.

The barn was on a big estate, and the estate belonged to an old Baron. The Baron came from a long line of very horsey people. He was wild about racing and wild about hunting, but wildest of all just about horses.

When the Baron's horses weren't being put through their paces for a race or being put through their paces for the hunt, the grooms rode them round and round in the great field beyond the cowshed. Some of the horses were trotters, some of them were pacers, and some of them just galloped, but all of them made loud clumping noises with their feet.

Hubert admired the horses very much. He envied the big important CLUMP, CLUMP noise they made. The truth was he wished he had been born a horse instead of a cat, though he didn't dare whisper this to anyone, not even to his friend Fayaway, the best of all the Baron's fine horses.

All the other cats were afraid of the horses. They would run and disappear into dark corners whenever the horses came into the barn.

They disappeared into dark corners whenever the old Baron came into the barn, too.
The Baron was big and fat and noisy, and
he hated anything that crept or slunk about
silently. Whenever he saw a cat, he would
make a terrible face and shout, "Scat!"

As the months went by and Hubert grew bigger and stronger, he began to imitate the horses. He stamped and pawed the ground. He put his head and tail up and his spine down and trotted around the barn. Then he galloped. But whenever he tried to pace, crossing one foot over the other, he got his paws all tangled up and fell on his chin.

And no matter how well he trotted and galloped, he made hardly any noise at all because his paws were soft. This made him so sad and melancholy that sometimes, when no one was looking, he would sit down and cry. But he never stopped practicing for long, and he grew more and more horsey every day.

Hubert's behavior bothered the other cats in his family. They would stop their mousing when he went by and glare at him from the shadows. Finally Hubert's father had a talk with him.

"A dog's a dog and a cat's a cat," Father told Hubert. "And a horse is a horse and a stooge of man, besides being the noisiest critter on earth. We cats have always been independent and silent. We're nervous and high strung. At least we're supposed to be."

"That's just it," said Hubert. "Cats have always been this and done that. Isn't it about time we changed? Isn't it time some of us forgot all that and made a big noise in the world?"

"Noise!" His father shuddered.

"It's time some cat stopped creeping and sneaking about and clumped when he walked —like this," Hubert said recklessly. And he threw his head and tail up and his spine down and pranced, bringing his feet down like the horses did.

"Ee-yowrr!" yowled Father Tom. He leaped straight up in the air and came down in his own tracks. So did Hubert's mother, Gray Mamma, and so did Striped Uncle and Big Brother who were nearby. For Hubert had indeed made a big noise—he had clumsily tipped over a leaning pitchfork that had fallen with a loud clang against a tin feed pan.

"Lightning cut you, boy!" squalled Striped Uncle, every hair on end. "My nerves won't take much more of this. You like to have scared me out of my last two lives!"

"Sorry, Unc," said Hubert. "But talking about being scared, it seems to me everyone around here acts scared most of the time. What is there to be afraid of, anyway? What keeps us all creeping and slinking around?"

"Great Dog, boy!" yowled Father. "We cats are silent because we have padded feet, not noisy hoofs. We're made that way so we can stalk a living."

"We don't have to stalk our living," said Hubert. "All we have to do is lie around till they bring us our milk and Grow Kat. We wouldn't get any more if we stalked all day. I get more than I can eat. I have to leave part of it for the rats and mice."

"You leave it for the rats and mice!" yelled Big Brother. "Why aren't you creeping up on them and killing them?"

"Why should I? I don't like them—to eat, that is."

"To eat, that is!" echoed Striped Uncle. "But otherwise they're all right! Just what do you like?"

"I like Grow Kat and I like horses," said Hubert, and he made a ruckling sound in his nostrils and stamped.

"I give up," said Striped Uncle. He slipped silently toward the shadows, with Big Brother following noiselessly along.

Hubert threw his head and tail up and his spine down and trotted the length of the barn.

"Look, son," said Gray Mamma nervously, "why don't you lie down and catnap, or play quietly with the tip of your tail like your brothers and sisters?"

Hubert snorted. "Cats have always slept, or played quietly with their tails. It's time

they did something different. It's time some-body *heard* them." He stamped several times and trotted off again.

Father clapped a paw to his head. "What have I ever done to be afflicted with a son like this? I'm off to the corn crib. There'll be no mousing here today."

Hubert came to a stop in the barn door-way. "Here come the horses," he called. "Look at the way they stride! Listen to them clump!"

The eight fine thoroughbreds that lived in the barn were coming down the lane from the tryout field. Hubert's special friend Fay-away, lovely red-brown Fayaway, was in the lead, a red-capped trainer in the saddle. Be-hind the horses came the fat, noisy old Baron himself.

The other cats in the barn disappeared into dark corners as usual when the horses came in, but Hubert marched out to meet them. Gray Mamma lingered last of all to gaze with grieving eyes at this smallest and strangest of her offspring. She saw him turn about and fall in with the horses. With head and tail up and spine down, he lifted his feet high and trotted along, trying to clump like they did. In all the dust and noise, no one except Mamma even noticed him.

An hour later all the horses had been rubbed down and fed, and the big barn was quiet again. Fayaway was munching his special measure of oats and timothy hay when Hubert trotted into the stall and jumped up to the manger for their evening talk. The two friends touched noses, and Fayaway told of the afternoon's happenings. Hubert took up a pawful of oats and munched, too. He had been sampling oats for a long time now and was getting to like them.

"It was just like all the other days this week," Fayaway said. "We raced five or six

times round the track, if you could call it racing — running with your own mother, brother, and sisters. I'll tell you something I wouldn't breathe to another soul: I feel sure I could have left them all behind if I'd had a chance, but that trainer kept reining me in till my mouth hurt."

"I know you could beat them all," Hubert

said. "They're holding you back because they're saving you for the big race."

"It's nice of you to say that," said Fayaway. "We can hope it's true. I admit that as a trotter in the shafts I've never been beaten."

"Trotting, that's for me," said Hubert. "I haven't missed a day practicing. I've even tried the pace."

"Wonderful. Persistence, that's what wins," said Fayaway. "Why don't you practice your gaits now? Maybe I can give you some pointers."

"Here goes," said Hubert. He jumped to the barn floor and began trotting back and forth, head and tail up, back down. He stamped and pawed. He galloped. But lift his

feet high and bring them down as he would, he made hardly any noise at all. Finally he tried to pace. As always, he stumbled and fell on his chin.

"Think nothing of it," said Fayaway. "It took me nearly six months to learn the pace —and it's still far from my best performance."

Despite his friend's encouragement, Hubert was so chagrined that he sat down in an empty stall and had a good waul.

Presently, two dull ruby gleams showed from a dark hole in a corner of the stall. It was old Ember Eye, king of the barn rats, watching from his secret hideout. The big gray rat came out and walked right up to Hubert with a toothy grin.

"What's the matter, young fellow? Don't they treat you right?" he asked in a wheezy whisper.

Hubert jumped and, without thinking, made a pass with his paw just like a regular cat. The old gray rat jerked back with a chatter of fear, and Hubert remembered that was no way for a horse to act.

"Sorry," he said contritely. "It was just a slip of the mind."

"Forget it," said the rat king. "No harm done. I came out to have a little talk with you."

Three other rats, all hard-looking characters, came out of the hole and gathered around Hubert.

"We've been watching you for a long time, and you're a right guy," said old Ember Eye. "You've never made a real pass at one of us. I want to thank you for that and for leaving a handout in your dish every day or two."

"Don't thank me," said Hubert. "I'm overfed around here anyhow. As for trying to kill a rat or mouse, I just can't see it."

"Are you kidding?" said the rat king.

"Honest. What would I want with a mouthful of rat? I'd rather eat Grow Kat and munch some oats—like a horse."

"So you're really set on being a horse," said the old rat with a hiccuppy laugh. "Well, boy, maybe we can help you out. Come on into the hideout."

Hubert followed Ember Eye and the other rats into a large gloomy hole beneath the floor.

The big rat popped some grains of the fat old Baron's corn into his mouth and then turned to Hubert.

"As I was saying, we've been watching
you a long time, and we want to see you go
right on acting like a horse and trying to
make all the noise you can. The more noise
you can make the more help you are to
us, understand? Where there's noise, there's
safety. It's these quiet characters like that
uncle of yours that are poison to us."

"Wait a minute," Hubert protested. "Unc
Stripes is—"

"Let me finish," ordered the head rat. "It's like this: you want to make noise and we can help you do it. All we want in return for helping you is your *good will*."

"Is it?" said Hubert.

"Of course." Old Ember Eye shifted closer to Hubert. "All we want is your friendship, boy," the rat said in a husky voice.

Hubert gulped shyly. "You've got it," he said.

They touched paws.

"Now, boy, lift up one of your feet," Ember Eye said. "We've got a little surprise for you."

Hubert did as he was told. He lifted one paw at a time, and within a few minutes the rats had fastened to his feet a set of heavy shoes they had made for him out of metal washers. Hubert stood up—and as he stood up he CLUMPED!

"There you are, boy," said Ember Eye. "You want to make a noise like a horse. You want to pace. Anybody knows you can't do it without horseshoes."

Hubert thanked Ember Eye and the other rats, touched paws all around, and hurried from the hideout. What a thrill it was to hear himself clump! He threw his head and tail up and his spine down and clumped through the barn with a racket that made his family jump for cover. They hissed at Hubert to be still so they could go on mousing, but Hubert went right on horsing. He tried the pace. This time he really did it because of the heavy shoes.

Back in their holes and crannies the rats squeaked and wheezed with laughter until they had to hold their sides.

All at once, Hubert threw his head up and neighed. Of course he neighed in a catty tone, but it was a pretty horsey neigh for a cat. Doubtless it was because of all the oats he had been eating.

Hubert's father had come back from the corn crib just in time to see and hear Hubert's whole performance. Hubert's neigh was the last straw. With his teeth bared and his eyes glaring, Father rushed at Hubert in a rage. Hubert saw him coming. Without thinking, he kicked out with both hind feet like a horse, and down went Father.

Poor Hubert. For the first time in his life he wanted to slink quietly to a dark corner. But he couldn't slink wearing his heavy metal shoes. He could only stand there, looking miserable.

"Did you see that, Mamma?" Father yowled, rubbing his shoulder. "He kicked me, just like a horse! He neighs like a horse and he makes noise enough for two horses. And now he kicks! If I hadn't seen it and felt it, I wouldn't believe it!"

"I saw him," Gray Mamma said, looking at Hubert with wide horrified eyes.

"Great Dog!" Father wauled. "I ask you, why was I ever afflicted with a son like this?"

"Oh, Tom!" Mamma said, and burst into tears.

"Son or no son, he's got to go!" Father railed. "Come on Brother, Uncle, get behind me!"

Big Brother and Striped Uncle came out of hiding, and the three of them advanced on Hubert in wedge formation.

"Wait, Pop—let me explain!" Hubert cried. But it was too late.

In less than a minute the three of them had rushed Hubert right out of the barn, down past the corn crib, and out beyond the cowshed. Then Father, Uncle, and Big Brother turned back toward the barn without even looking around. But Hubert did. After he had clumped another hundred feet, he looked back again. And when he had clumped five hundred feet he looked back a third time and wauled. Then he sat down in the weeds to think.

He had never dreamed that things would come to this! He'd been driven out of family,

house, and home, even out of contact with Fayaway, his best friend. He finally decided he'd have to live in the cowshed.

For a while Hubert was lonely and un-happy, but he soon had the cowshed rats for friends. And even though he went right on practicing his paces, his family didn't stay angry with him for long. They wouldn't let him come back to live in the barn and ruin their mousing with his clumping about, but they did stop by to talk with him out in the barn lot. Now and then, when Father was away, Gray Mamma would invite Hubert into the barn for a visit. Some of those times Hubert was able to have a few words with his friend Fayaway.

The day of the big trotting race came round, and Fayaway won the race just as Hubert had thought he would. After that, whenever Fayaway was ridden home from practice, Hubert would run proudly along beside him, either trotting or pacing, right up to the barn door.

One day the fat old Baron saw Hubert clumping along the lane, and he laughed so

hard and so long that he had to be held up by two grooms or he would have fallen to the ground. The Baron was getting so old and so fat that he rarely rode a horse any more. Besides that, he ate so much rich food that he had the gout, and most days he couldn't go outdoors at all. He was miserable because he couldn't bring his horses right into the house. When he saw Hubert clumping about, he decided to bring him in instead.

The Baron had a small race track built in his great hall for Hubert to train on, and he appointed a special groom for Hubert. When Hubert tired of trotting and galloping and pacing, the groom would put him in a little stall and strap a blanket around him and feed him a small measure of oats with his Grow Kat while the Baron laughed and laughed.

Hubert was so happy in the house with the fat, noisy old Baron that he hardly ever bothered to go outdoors any more. The old Baron hardly ever went outdoors any more, either. He could watch his horses from the window, and he was just as happy in the house with Hubert as Hubert was with him.

The Baron didn't have any sons and he didn't have any daughters and he hadn't had a wife for a long time. He just had Hubert.

All this happened a long time ago, and Hubert has grown up long since. He still lives in the Baron's house, and he is married now. He married just an ordinary catty cat, and three of his children are just ordinary catty cats. But the fourth takes after his father and is the horsiest kind of cat imaginable.